GEORGE ROGERS CLARK

BOY OF THE NORTHWEST FRONTIER

Written by
Katharine E. Wilkie

Illustrated by
Cathy Morrison

Patria Press, Inc.
PO Box 752
Carmel IN 46082
www.patriapress.com

Printed and bound in the United States of America
10 9 8 7 6 5 4 3 2 1

Text originally published by the Bobbs-Merrill Company, 1974, in the
Childhood of Famous Americans Series® The Childhood of Famous Americans
Series® is a registered trademark of Simon & Schuster, Inc.

Library of Congress Cataloging-in-Publication Data

Wilkie, Katharine Elliott, 1904-1980
   George Rogers Clark, boy of the Northwest frontier / written by
Katharine E. Wilkie ; illustrated by Cathy Morrison.
      p. cm. — (Young patriots series ; 8)
   Summary: Childhood of the explorer and soldier who won the Northwest
Territory for the United States during the Revolutionary War.
   ISBN 1-882859-44-8 (pbk.) — ISBN 1-882859-43-X (hardcover)
   1. Clark, George Rogers, 1752-1818—Childhood and youth—Juvenile
literature. 2. Frontier and pioneer life—Northwest, Old—Juvenile
literature. 3. Pioneer children—Northwest, Old—Biography—Juvenile
literature. 4. Northwest, Old—History—To 1775—Juvenile literature. 5.
Northwest, Old—Biography—Juvenile literature. 6. Generals—United
States—Biography—Juvenile literature. [1. Clark, George Rogers,
1752-1818—Childhood and youth. 2. Frontier and pioneer life—Northwest,
Old. 3. Generals.] I. Morrison, Cathy, ill. II. Title. III. Series.

E207.C5 W49 2004
973.3'3'092—dc22   2003018782

Edited by Harold Underdown
Design by inari

Contents

Illustrations

Dedication

To Raymond with love

*Publisher's Note: The term "Indian" for Native Americans
was commonly used and accepted during the time of
George Rogers Clark. It is not our intention to offend any ethnic
group by its use in the text. We have kept it in the story as we feel
it is important to stay historically accurate and true
to the time period portrayed.*

Books in the Young Patriots Series

Watch for more **Young Patriots** Coming Soon
Visit www.patriapress.com for updates!

Chapter 1

Goodbye to the Mountains

On a cold Virginia morning in 1757, five-year-old George Rogers Clark went over to the first of the two wagons in front of his family's house. His father was adjusting the harness on the lead horse.

"Why do we have to leave Albemarle County?" George asked again. "I'm not afraid of Indians."

John Clark looked at his second son. "I've told you," he said. "It will be safer back in Caroline County. That's just good sense."

"But there won't be mountains, you said."

"And there won't be Indian attacks, either," his father interrupted.

George ignored this. "Tom Jefferson won't be there."

"I forgot!" his father exclaimed suddenly. "I forgot to ride over with the receipt for the money Mrs.

Jefferson paid me for that horse last week."

"I could take it!" George said eagerly.

Jonathan, George's older brother, poked his head out of the front of the wagon. "Do you want me to take it for you, Father?" Jonathan called.

George had already mounted his black pony, Soldier.

"Thanks, Jonathan," their father said. "But George is ready, so he may as well go." He reached in his pocket and pulled out a piece of paper.

"Now I'll get to see Tom again!" George said. Eagerly he turned the pony toward the gate.

"Wait," his father called. "Didn't you forget something?"

George looked back. His father stood with the receipt still held in his outstretched hand. George laughed and rode back to get it.

Mr. Clark hid a smile as his son took the receipt. "You might not have to ride all the way to Shadwell," he said. "I heard Tom say he might go to the mill today. Stop by to see whether he's there. And hurry."

"I will." George started away.

John Clark watched his son ride down the road. George sat his pony well.

Jonathan yelled after George, "Be careful!"

George turned in the saddle and waved.

Sometimes he thought his older brother worried about him as much as his father did.

Soldier broke into a faster gait. His father had given George the pony for his fourth birthday, on November 19, 1756. In a year George had learned to ride as well as many adults.

The wind whipped at the young rider's face. It was a brisk December wind, but George liked the way it stung his cheeks.

When he had gone about a mile he came to the mill. The large paddle wheel turned steadily in the stream. A horse stood tied to a rail in front. George was disappointed when he saw that the horse was Tom Jefferson's. Now he had no reason to ride all the way to Shadwell.

"Well, George Rogers!" Tom Jefferson, a tall boy in his early teens, came out the door.

George swung to the ground. "I have something for your mother." He handed the receipt to Tom. "It's for the horse."

Tom took it and smiled.

"Father almost forgot," George said.

"Mother always says your father's word is as good as a receipt," Tom replied.

Tom went to the hitching rail where his horse was tied. "I'll ride back with you," he said. "I want to tell your folks goodbye."

George quickly climbed up on Soldier. "Race!" he cried. And he was off down the road. He bent low and let the pony run. The pony's hoofs pounded on the frozen earth.

When he could hear Tom's horse coming up even with him, George let Soldier slow down. Tom always gave George a head start when they raced. George usually went full speed until Tom passed him. But he didn't want to hurry now. The family would be ready to leave by the time he got back.

Tom rode up beside him.

"I wish you were coming with us, Tom," George said.

Tom smoothed his horse's mane. "I'll miss riding over from Shadwell every week."

"Can you come to take me fishing sometime?" George asked. "After we move, there won't be anyone to teach me."

"You couldn't find a better woodsman than your father," Tom said. "He can tell you more about fishing and tracking and trail blazing than I ever could."

"Yes," George agreed. "But he's too busy to go out with me very much. And anyway, I learn more when you explain things."

"Well, maybe you can come back here for a visit," Tom said.

When he could hear Tom's horse coming even with him,
George let Soldier slow down.

"How will you know when I'm coming?"

"Why, I'll just watch for that red hair of yours," Tom chuckled. "I'll be able to see you five miles off."

George laughed. Tom Jefferson's hair was as red as George's. The two boys often joked together about the color of their hair.

Soon the boys turned into the trampled path where the Clark wagons and livestock stood.

Mr. and Mrs. Clark came out of the house. George's younger sister, Ann, marched after them.

"That was a fast trip," Mr. Clark said. "How are you, Tom?"

"Well, I'd feel better if all of you weren't leaving," Tom answered. He dismounted and took baby John in his arms while Mr. Clark helped Mrs. Clark onto the high wagon seat. Mr. Clark climbed up on the seat beside his wife. Then Tom handed up the baby.

George went around to help three-year-old Ann get into the back of the wagon. Tom took his horse's reins. "We're going to miss you," he said. He reached up and shook hands with Mr. Clark.

"Tell your mother we send our best regards. We hope to see her soon," Mrs. Clark said.

"And tell her we wish the Jeffersons would move back to the Tidewater with us," added Mr. Clark.

Mrs. Clark leaned across her husband and took Tom's hand. "Take care of your mother and the girls. And remember, the door will always be open for you at our house."

"I'll come if I can," Tom answered. "But it's a two-day trip, and I'm pretty busy these days. As Mother says, I'm the man of the family now." Tom's father had died a few months before.

The horses tugged at the reins till the wagons started rolling. After one more goodbye, Tom headed back to the Jefferson plantation.

Mr. Clark cracked his whip over the horses' heads. "Good-by, mountains," he sang out. "We're on our way. Lead on, George!"

For days George had been looking forward to leading the procession. Soldier pranced and danced. George sat up straight in the saddle. The wagons began to roll.

Jonathan rode in the second wagon with York, one of the family's slaves. York let him drive. Ann snuggled under a bearskin rug in the first wagon.

George turned in his saddle and looked back to make sure everything was right. Jonathan waved and yelled, "Lead the way, George!"

"We should be halfway there by nightfall," his father called out.

The morning passed slowly for most of the family. There seemed to be no end to the pines and oaks on either side of the rough road. Only now and then

For days George had been looking forward to leading
the procession.

did they see a settler's cabin.

But George liked the woods. The journey went
too quickly for him. Sometimes he rode ahead like

an advance scout. Then he would come back and tell them that all was clear ahead.

At midday the family stopped for a meal. York built a fire of brush and dry limbs. George helped York gather the wood. As soon as they had eaten, they were on their way again.

George looked around at the trees. Then he looked at the miles of country stretching out ahead. He felt proud to be leading his family through the woods to their new home.

That night they camped by the trail. It was the best part of the trip for George. He had never camped out overnight before. The flickering campfire made exciting shadows in the trees.

After supper everyone went to bed in the wagons. They went to sleep early, because they wanted to start out again as soon as the sun rose. They had another long journey ahead of them tomorrow.

George was as eager the next morning as he had been on the first day. Though the weather had turned colder, it didn't bother him.

But as evening came on, even George felt the cold. He was hungry, too. Baby John began to cry. George heard Mother try to comfort him. Ann gave an unhappy sniffle now and then. Even Jonathan complained a little.

The baby's cries became so loud that Mr. Clark stopped the wagons. George halted Soldier and walked back to the front wagon. He reached up and put something in his mother's hand.

"What's this?" she asked.

"Some barley sugar," George said. "I was saving

it for myself, but John likes it, too."

"That's nice of you," his mother said. "Thank you, George."

George looked ahead, trying to see through the darkness.

"Look, Father!" he shouted suddenly. "What's that?" He pointed to a spot of light that shone faintly on a distant hill.

"Where?" his father asked. It was too dark for him to see George's pointing finger.

"Over there," George cried. "See?"

"Why, I think that's our new home!" his father said. "I hope Dilsey and Harry have everything ready for us."

Dilsey and her husband were slaves who had worked for the Clark family for a long time. They had gone ahead two days before to get the house ready.

George forgot his cold feet and hands. "I'll ride ahead and tell them we're coming!" he shouted. He nudged Soldier's flanks with his heels. The pony broke into a canter.

The moon peeked through the clouds, and George could see the trail plainly. In a short while he came to a lane that branched off the main road. Soldier was winded now and trotted slowly up the hill.

As soon as he reached the big house, George slid

from the pony's back. He ran to the door, threw it open, and rushed in.

It was a real plantation house. The big room had a high-beamed ceiling. There was a cheery fire blazing on the hearth. George could tell he was going to like his new home.

Suddenly he smelled hot food.

"Dilsey!" he yelled. His face felt funny when he moved his mouth. The cold had made his face stiff, and now the heat made it tingle.

Dilsey came out from the kitchen. "Mercy on us! Close that door, Mister George, before we all freeze to death," she said.

She pulled him over to the hearth and began to unbutton his coat. He didn't like being fussed over, and he twisted away. "I'm hungry!" he said. "We're all hungry. The others will be here right away!"

Dilsey chuckled. "We're ready for you."

George said, "If you'd looked, you'd have known a long time ago that we were coming."

"Now, how would I have known that?"

"Why, you can see my red hair five miles off!" he laughed.

An hour later all the Clarks were sitting around the fireplace in their new home. Mr. Clark had just thrown another log on the flames. Dilsey had served them a good supper. The baby was asleep in his cradle. The warmth of the room felt good after the long, cold trip.

"Back in the Virginia Tidewater at last," George's mother said, sounding pleased. "Now I will see my parents and my brothers and sisters more often."

"And George will meet the uncle he's named after," his father added.

"I'd like that," said George.

"We'll go for a visit soon," his father said. "Uncle George and Aunt Frances have two boys, you know—Joseph and John. Maybe they'll go camping with you, George."

George didn't answer. He wasn't sure that camping with his cousins would be like camping with Tom Jefferson. He wasn't sure that anything here would be like the foothills in Albemarle County.

His father noticed his solemn face. "Never mind, son. Caroline County is a fine place to hunt and fish, too. There are miles and miles of forest around here."

George's face brightened. "Good," he said.

He watched the dancing flames in the fireplace. He grew sleepy. He thought about all these forests he had never seen. There would be lots of things to explore. He yawned and closed his eyes.

Chapter 2

The Best Medicine

George didn't know what was wrong with Ann, but he had heard his mother say something about "fever." For the last week Ann had rested on the couch by the fireplace. But for a week before that she had been in bed. The family had been at their new home for over a year, and this was the first time that any of them had been seriously ill.

This spring morning George and Jonathan were just finishing one of Dilsey's good breakfasts. The boys drank the last of their milk and went into the sitting room. Their mother was reading to Ann and little John. Their father had already gone out for an early-morning ride over the plantation.

George looked at Ann lying on the couch. He felt strange when he saw how pale and quiet she was. She used to run and laugh all the time.

Their mother was different since Ann had become sick. She was quiet and sighed a lot. George wished Ann would get well.

"Where are you two going?" their mother asked.

"We're going to look for raccoons!" George said.

"You weren't supposed to tell," Jonathan said. He poked his younger brother.

Their mother frowned. George was afraid she might say they couldn't go. Since Ann had fallen sick their mother seemed to worry more about them.

Suddenly Ann began to whimper.

Their mother got up and went over to the couch. "What's wrong, dear?" she asked. She smoothed Ann's hair.

Ann didn't answer. She buried her face in the quilt and went on whimpering.

Their mother picked up Ann's corncob doll. "Don't you want to play with Julia?" she asked. Julia was Ann's favorite doll.

"No," Ann cried. "Julia's sick."

"Well, we'd better nurse her and get her well."

"She's too sick," Ann replied.

All this carrying on made George restless. "Let's go," he said to Jonathan.

As they went out the door, Mother said, "Do your chores before you go. And be back in time for lunch."

George and Jonathan cut the firewood and carried it to the kitchen. Then they headed across the south meadow for the woods.

The woods were just turning green. Most of the trees had large buds that would soon become leaves. The spring rains had made the ground soft with mud and matted dead leaves.

George was bursting with excitement. It was hard for Jonathan to keep up with him. Jonathan liked the woods, but not as much as George did. Jonathan followed and occasionally pointed out an easier path.

"Nat Strong shouldn't have shot a mother raccoon," Jonathan said. Nat Strong was the oldest boy of the neighboring family who lived about a mile east of the Clarks.

"That's what I told him, when I saw him shoot her yesterday," George answered. "I told him there would be babies in the tree."

"I hope we can still get the babies," Jonathan said. "They make good pets."

"There's the raccoon tree!" George pointed at an enormous oak tree. "Let's climb it."

"What!" exclaimed Jonathan. "How are you going to climb a tree that big? We need a rope or something."

"I didn't think of that," George said.

They went over to the tree and walked around it. The first limbs were too high to reach, even if one of them stood on the other's shoulders.

"Look!" George cried. He pointed at a hollow in the tree about twenty feet from the ground. "That's where the nest is."

"That's way up!" Jonathan said.

George ran and stretched his arms around the tree trunk. They didn't reach halfway. He put the soles of his shoes against the rough bark and tried to push himself up. But he lost his grip and fell back in the mud.

Jonathan came over to help him up. He brushed at the mud on George's back. "You'll never get up that way." He laughed.

George looked with disgust at the tree. "How can we climb it?"

Jonathan tilted his head back. He squinted at the high limbs. "Can't climb it without a ladder," he said finally.

George sat down on a stump. "There aren't any ladders out here," he said sadly. "And we couldn't bring one from home very easily."

Jonathan was thinking. "Maybe we could make one," he said. "Remember that windbreak we made near here? We could get some of those long poles we cut for the windbreak and make a ladder with. . . ."

But he was talking to the tree. George was racing toward the windbreak that he and Jonathan had built for shelter against wind gusts.

At the windbreak, George hunted around until he found the extra poles they had cut. There were three of them. Two were small and crooked, but the biggest one was about right. It was a long, straight sapling about four inches thick and fifteen feet long.

By the time Jonathan came up, George had begun to drag the pole toward the oak tree. "Come on," George grunted. "Help me."

Jonathan grabbed the other end and helped carry the pole. "Now what?" he asked.

"We'll lay it up against that fork," George said. He pointed at the main fork in the tree, about five feet above their heads. "And I'll climb it."

"You can't climb that pole," Jonathan said. "It's dead. It will break."

"No, it won't," George answered.

Jonathan disagreed, but he helped to lay one end of the pole in the fork. Then Jonathan stood on the lower end. "It will break," he warned again.

George took hold of the pole from underneath and swung his feet up to lock around it. Then his muddy shoes slipped, and he was left hanging by his hands. Crack went the pole. George dropped to the ground.

"You could climb better barefoot," Jonathan said. "But I still think the pole will break."

George was already taking off his shoes and

stockings. "No, it won't," he answered. He started to climb again. Without shoes his feet didn't slip, but it was hard work to climb that way.

The pole bent, cracked, and popped. Jonathan yelled, "It's breaking! It's breaking!" George hurried to get to the fork before the pole broke, and skinned his hands and feet.

Then he reached the fork and pulled himself into the tree. "I did it!" he cried.

"You're just lucky!" Jonathan called.

The big limbs of the oak made the rest of the climb easy. In a short while George was able to peer into the raccoon's hole.

"What do you see?" Jonathan called.

"They're in there, I think," George yelled. Carefully he stuck his arm in the hole, all the way to the shoulder. "I can reach them!"

It was hard for Jonathan to tell what George was doing. It looked as if he was taking things out of the hole and then putting them back. "Did you get them?" he called.

"Wait a minute." George started back down to the fork. He used only one hand to climb. With the other hand he held something close against his chest.

When he reached the fork, George took off his coat and put something in the pocket. Then he lowered the coat to Jonathan by one sleeve.

"Be careful," George said. "That's the only one that was alive."

Jonathan took the coat and peered into the pocket. Then he stood on the end of the pole so that it wouldn't slip.

George started down, and the pole creaked and cracked and bent more than ever. When he was halfway down it broke with a sudden snap. He went sprawling in the mud.

"I knew it would break," Jonathan said. "Are you hurt?"

"No," George said. "I'm all right. Let me see the raccoon." He took the tiny grayish-brown animal in his hands. It moved its legs helplessly.

"It sure is a little one," George said.

"It doesn't look very healthy," Jonathan observed. "It can hardly move."

"It's all right," George said. "It'll make a good pet."

They started back through the woods. It was past noon by now, and the day had turned warm.

The sun shone in a clear sky. George tramped through the woods at his brother's side. He felt good. He was covered with mud, but he had a raccoon.

When they got home, Ann cried and their mother sighed. Ann cried because she wanted the little raccoon as soon as she saw it, and George said it was his. Their mother sighed because George was covered with mud.

George stood holding the little raccoon happily, and wishing he hadn't gotten so muddy.

"I want it! I want it!" Ann cried pitifully. Tears streamed down her pale face.

"I'll tell you what," their mother said to comfort her. "I'll make you a new dress."

"I don't want a dress!" Ann shrieked. "I want the 'coon!"

"But it's George's raccoon. He had to go way out in the woods and catch it."

Ann just wailed.

George walked over to his little sister. He wished she'd stop crying and get well.

Little John, who had been playing in the corner, began to cry, too. He did everything Ann did. He even cried when she did.

"Here," George said. He held out the baby raccoon to Ann. "I'll give it to you. But you'll have to take care of it. It's awfully little."

George put the furry little raccoon in her hands. The warmth of the house seemed to have revived it, and it wiggled excitedly.

Ann stopped crying.

She looked at George silently with big wet eyes. Gently her little fingers stroked the raccoon's gray fur.

He could hear Ann humming a lullaby and rocking her doll Julia gently in her arms.

Suddenly she hugged the raccoon tightly with one arm and threw the other around George's neck.

"Look out!" George cried as he backed away. "You'll squash it."

Ann giggled and sat up with the baby raccoon in her lap.

That afternoon George and Jonathan built a box for the raccoon. Then they helped Ann feed it some milk. It couldn't drink by itself and they had to feed it from a spoon.

Late that night, after everyone was in bed, there was a noise in the sitting room. Their parents got up to see what it was.

George and Jonathan came out of their upstairs room and went halfway down the stairs. From there they could see into the room.

The fire had burned down to bright coals in the big fireplace. Ann knelt by the box with the little raccoon in it. She was covering it with a piece of cloth.

When Ann heard her mother and father she looked up. "I must keep it warm," she said. "It's so little."

Their mother said softly, "But you've been sick. You should be in bed."

"No," Ann said. "I feel good." She smiled. Her face was bright and cheerful.

"I think George brought home some good medicine today," their father said softly.

"Some very good medicine," their mother agreed.

George was glad he had given Ann the baby raccoon. He could hear Ann humming a lullaby and rocking her doll Julia gently in her arms. Then Ann stopped humming. "Look, Mother," she said. "Julia's well."

The Secret Tunnel

"**N**o wood to chop!" George cried happily as he ran from the house.

"No hens to feed!" Jonathan added.

Their father came out of the house, carrying a small trunk. "Well, I'm glad to see you two are so pleased to go on a visit."

"We're all ready," Jonathan said.

The Clarks were going to visit George Rogers, the uncle for whom George was named. Uncle George lived on a plantation on the eastern edge of Caroline County. The Clark and Rogers families often visited each other.

"If someone would get the other trunk, we would be almost ready to go," their father said.

"We'll get it," Jonathan said. He and George hurried toward the house. They were anxious to get started.

Half an hour later all the family was in the wagon.

Their parents sat up front. Their mother held the new baby, Richard, in her arms. Jonathan, George and Ann sat in the back among the trunks and bundles. They sang songs to pass the time away. Their little brother John, whom Ann was holding, tried to join in the singing.

Late that afternoon the Clarks pulled into the lane that led to Uncle George's house. Uncle George and his family and some guests were sitting on the green lawn. When they saw the Clarks, they all began to wave.

The wagon stopped and the Clarks climbed down. Uncle George and Aunt Frances hurried forward. Mrs. Clark and Aunt Frances greeted each other with loud exclamations. It had been a whole month since they had seen each other.

Mr. Clark and Uncle George shook hands heartily. Then they walked over to the other men and at once began to talk about crops.

Ann went with her mother to join the women. Four-year-old John followed his father and Uncle George.

The two Rogers boys, John and Joseph, led George and Jonathan toward the house. Joseph was bursting with news. "Hurry," he said. "We have something to show you."

"What?" asked George.

Joseph turned to his two cousins. "You remember that secret tunnel that runs from the cellar down to the orchard?"

"Oh, that," said George. "Can we go through it? I thought Uncle George told you to stay out of there."

"He did," Joseph replied. "But that's not what I mean. We found something else."

"Do you remember that other door in the cellar?" John asked. "It was bolted on the other side, and we wondered where it went."

"It's a secret passage!" Joseph blurted. "From upstairs down to the cellar."

"How did you find it?" George asked.

"We heard Father say there was a secret passage," Joseph answered. "So John and I looked for it the other day. And I pushed on the wall, and there it was!"

"Where is it?" George asked eagerly. "Let's go through it now!"

"We better not," said Jonathan. "These old passages were built a long time ago to use for escaping if Indians surrounded the house. The wood's probably rotten now."

"That's what Father said when we heard him talk about it," John said. "He didn't know we were around. He'd skin us alive if he knew we'd been through it—and the stairs really are rotten."

"Well, we can go through the tunnel then," said George.

Jonathan looked at his brother with a pained expression. "You know what Uncle George said. That tunnel's dangerous. Those old walls might cave in on us."

"I don't think it's that dangerous," John said. "I'll ask Father if we can go through it tomorrow when we have our old clothes on. Maybe we can sneak a look at the passage, too."

"All right," said Jonathan. "But I'm still not sure it's a good idea."

"We go through it all the time. Father just doesn't know it," Joseph added.

"Let's go in," John said. "I'm hungry, and it's almost time to eat."

All the boys were hungry. They hurried to the back sitting room. Ann was there, playing on the floor with another little girl.

"When do we eat?" asked Jonathan.

"We'll eat as soon as the grownups have been served," Joseph said.

From the dining room came the sound of laughter and tinkling glasses. The smell of rich food made the boys' mouths water.

"I hope they hurry," said George.

"My stomach is sticking to my backbone," John Rogers said. He rubbed his stomach.

Suddenly Joseph tapped his brother on the shoulder. "Look," he said softly. He pointed toward the back hallway.

All the boys looked through the doorway that led to the back hall. The late afternoon sun shone faintly through the windows.

The boys could see a man in the shadowed corner of the hall. He was flattened against the wall as if he wanted to hide.

"Who is it?" Joseph whispered.

John squinted. "I don't know. Not one of the guests. None of them would be in the back hall."

"Look!" said George. "Where's he going?"

The man had inched over to the stairs and started up on tiptoe.

John gasped. "I think I recognized him."

"Me, too," Joseph said.

John looked at his brother. "It's Mr. Warren." Then he turned to explain to George and Jonathan. "Mr. Warren's a planter who has come to buy horses for his stables. He's been here with us all week. He bought some horses from Father."

"But why isn't he at the table?" Joseph asked.

"I don't know," John replied. "It's funny, isn't it?"

"We'd better see what he's doing."

The boys slipped quietly into the hall and started up the stairs. The two little girls started to follow, but the boys motioned them back.

"I'll go ahead and watch him," George whispered. "I can move without making much noise."

With that, he moved away as swiftly and quietly as a shadow.

At the top of the stairs George dropped to his knees and peered around the corner into the upstairs hall. Then he turned and beckoned the others to follow. They came up behind him. "He went down the hall. He's looking in all the rooms," George whispered.

They all leaned out and looked. Mr. Warren had reached the room at the head of the front stairs. He glanced behind him. The boys ducked.

"That's the room where Father keeps his money," whispered John.

"The money Mr. Warren paid Father for the horses is in there," Joseph said aloud.

"Shhh!" Jonathan cautioned. "Talk softly or he'll hear us."

"We'd better warn Father," John whispered.

"Let's see what Mr. Warren is doing first," Jonathan whispered back. "We'd look pretty silly if we were wrong."

They looked around the corner again. Mr. Warren had disappeared. The boys slipped quietly into the hall and crept toward the room. John peeked in the door cautiously. Mr. Warren was fumbling with the lid of a metal strongbox.

John jerked back and hissed to his brother, "Go get Father!"

"You spying little puppies!" a deep voice boomed. Mr. Warren stood in the doorway, with a money bag in his left hand and a pistol in his right. It was the biggest, meanest-looking pistol George had ever seen.

"Run!" cried John. But the boys stood frozen with fright.

George felt as if he couldn't breathe. What could they do? Suddenly he put his head down and lunged forward. His head hit Mr. Warren's stomach. He felt the man double up and heard the pistol go off.

The money bag fell to the floor. George grabbed it and scrambled to his feet. He was surprised to see that John had the gun. George had knocked it from the man's hand without knowing it.

"Run, George!" John shouted. "Get Father!"

Mr. Warren closed in on them again.

"Shoot!" George cried.

Instead, John ran to the open window and threw the pistol outside.

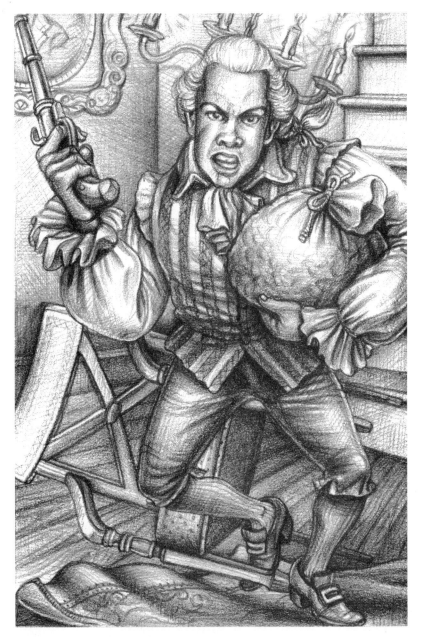

Mr. Warren stood in the doorway, with a money bag in his left hand and a pistol in his right.

George backed toward the doorway. Jonathan and Joseph turned and ran for the stairs. But George and John were cut off.

"Father!" George yelled. "Uncle George!"

Like a huge bear, Mr. Warren dived. George ducked back into the bedroom. Mr. Warren crashed against the door frame.

George heard John say, "This way! Quick!"

George looked in amazement. John had swung open a panel in the wall. There was the secret passage!

George just had time to lunge through the narrow opening. Mr. Warren caught John and threw him to the floor with a crash.

George had no time to close the panel behind him. He stumbled headlong down the narrow stairs, clutching the money bag to his chest with sweaty hands. Mr. Warren's heavy footsteps thudded behind him.

Suddenly he heard the sound of splintering wood and a crash. The rotten stairs had given way under Mr. Warren's weight. George went faster. Now there was at least a chance for him to get away.

Because of the darkness, George banged into the door at the bottom at full speed. He was stunned for a moment. Then he grappled frantically with the heavy beam that barred the door. At last he raised it and swung the door back. He could hear Mr. Warren again, crashing down the stairs.

George burst into the cellar and ran across the earth floor. He recognized the heavy oak door on the other side as the entrance to the tunnel. What if it was barred?

Holding the money bag tightly, George pushed at the great door. It opened with terrifying slowness. Mr. Warren had almost reached the bottom of the stairs. The door was still barely open when George wiggled through into the tunnel.

He could hear Mr. Warren race heavily across the floor. He dropped the bag, and with all his strength pushed the door shut. He pulled at the thick oak beam that would bar it, and the beam fell into place with a crash.

George sighed with relief. Then Mr. Warren was at the door. He pounded so hard that dirt and rotten wood from the door fell like rain at George's feet.

Then the pounding stopped. George listened intently. The adults must have been warned by now or have heard all the noise that he and Mr. Warren had made. Why hadn't they come? George heard nothing on the other side of the door.

Where was Mr. Warren? What was he doing? Then George had a frightening thought. Mr.

Warren might have a partner. The partner could be keeping the adults under guard while Mr. Warren stole the money. John hadn't said anything about anyone else. But if someone was helping him, then Mr. Warren could take his time to catch George. Right now Mr. Warren might be headed for the other end of the tunnel. He might not know where it went. But if he did, George was trapped.

George's heart pounded. He decided he had to follow the tunnel and hope he reached the orchard first. He couldn't go back to the cellar. Mr. Warren might be waiting. Once he opened the door, George wouldn't have a chance.

George picked up the money bag and started down the tunnel. He wished Jonathan was with him.

The tunnel was dark, but George moved as fast as he could. He looked down and couldn't see his feet. He guided himself by brushing along the wall with his shoulder.

At last he saw a glimmer of light. The floor of the tunnel grew slippery. The spring in the orchard, near the tunnel entrance, kept the earth damp. He was coming to the end.

George stopped. He took deep breaths of fresh air. The air farther back in the tunnel had been stale and damp. Would it be better to wait inside?

George picked up the money bag and started
down the tunnel.

Or should he take a chance that Mr. Warren hadn't
found the opening yet? If not, George would have a
good chance to get away into the woods. He decided
to try it.

George rushed from the tunnel. He blinked. Even the late afternoon light hurt his eyes after the darkness of the tunnel. Then he blinked even more. He couldn't believe what he saw.

The men and boys from the house were coming to meet him. His father and Uncle George headed the party. Jonathan, Joseph, and John Rogers were close behind. They swarmed around him like bees. "Are you all right?" his father asked anxiously.

"I'm fine," George gasped. He tried to keep his legs from shaking.

His uncle threw an arm around George's shoulders. "You're a brave boy. I'm proud to have you for a namesake. But you shouldn't have worried about the money."

"What?" George asked.

"The money," his uncle said. He pointed at the money bag which George was still holding. "You shouldn't have worried about that. The important thing was to get yourself out."

"Oh!" George exclaimed. In the excitement he had not remembered the money bag.

"But I thank you with all my heart," said Uncle George.

Then George saw John. "Did Mr. Warren hurt you?" he asked his cousin.

"No, not much," John replied. "He was too interested in the money to waste time with me." He grinned at George. "I'm glad you had the money bag, and not me."

"How did you know I was in the tunnel?"

"Father and Uncle George found Mr. Warren by the door in the cellar," Jonathan replied. "That's where they caught him."

"After the boys let us out of the dining room," Uncle George said.

"Warren's servant locked us in," George's father explained. "He threatened to shoot anyone who tried to break out. He was holding a gun on the servants in the kitchen when we caught up with him."

"Then someone was helping him," George said. "It's a good thing Jonathan and Joseph got away to let you out."

"You all did a job," Uncle George said. "But you saved the money, George. Though it was a foolhardy thing to do, I'm proud of you."

George felt embarrassed, but proud. "Where's Mr. Warren now?" he asked.

"Trussed up like a turkey in the cellar," his father said grimly.

"He told me he was a planter," Uncle George said with disgust. "And he was nothing but a common horse-trading thief. Well, he and his 'servant' will be on their way to jail in Fredericksburg tomorrow."

One of the men from the crowd said, "You certainly used your head, George."

George smiled. Now that it was over, the chase seemed funny in a way. "I only used my head once," George said. "Mostly I used my feet." At that, everyone laughed. And George laughed harder than anyone else.

Chapter 4

A Knife and a Name

Geoorge woke early one fall morning. He rolled over and looked out the window. The sky was gray and filled with thunderclouds.

In spite of the weather, George felt good. He yawned and stretched. He seemed to tingle inside. Today he and his father would begin their trip to Albemarle County.

His father had talked about selling the old Albemarle farm to Josiah Lawrence. Josiah lived near the mountains, close to Indian territory.

Jonathan was staying at home. He was the oldest boy, so it was his responsibility to care for the family when their father was away. Jonathan had beamed with pride when their father said that.

For George the trip was a reward. He was still a sort of hero. Everyone talked about how he had outwitted the thief and saved the money. His father had said George deserved a reward. And George couldn't think of a better one than a trip back to the mountains.

George dressed in a hurry and rushed downstairs. Mr. Clark wanted to make an early start so they could get to Mr. Lawrence's the next afternoon.

George's parents were eating breakfast when he came in. The other children were not up yet.

"Good morning, George," his mother said.

His father grinned and cut into a corncake. "No one had to get you up this morning, I see."

"I woke up almost before daylight."

Dilsey came over and set a big plate of eggs on the table. "You'd better eat a lot." She smiled. "It's a long, hungry trip back to the mountains."

George looked around the food-laden table. There were eggs, done just right, golden-brown corncakes and pewter mugs of cool milk.

After breakfast, George and his father put what supplies they needed in their saddlebags. York saddled their horses. When they were ready, his mother, Ann, and Jonathan came out to say goodby.

As they rode off, Rex, George's hound, ran after them. His father had given him Rex to be his hunting dog when Princess, his father's hunting dog, had pups. George had to stop and get off his horse to send the dog back. Rex had grown into a fine hound.

His father set a steady pace. A medium speed was best for a long trip, he said. You could make the best time that way without tiring the horses.

"I wish I was going to see Tom Jefferson," George said.

"I'm afraid his studies take all his time," his father replied. "He's in Williamsburg this year."

They jogged along, George excited as always at riding through the woods. They had some food in their saddlebags. George had a bow and arrows, and his father had a Deckard, a long-barreled rifle made in Pennsylvania. They would kill game along the way and cook it over a campfire that night.

"Father," George said suddenly. "Do I seem older than I am?"

His father looked up, startled. "Well, sometimes, yes. Why?"

"Sometimes I feel older."

"Well, you're big for your age. And you're strong. You can outwrestle practically everybody your age in Caroline County. Most of the time you get the better of Jonathan, even though he's two years older. But Jonathan takes to books a lot better than you."

"That's right," George agreed. He knew Jonathan not only read well but could remember everything that he read. "But he doesn't know as much about the woods as I do," George added. "He doesn't care as much, either."

His father laughed. "I guess you're just a born woodsman, George. You may get that from your great-grandfather Giles. He was a frontiersman. He had the wilderness in his blood, your Uncle George always says."

George thought about that a moment. Then he said, "I think I have, too."

All day they traveled along the road that led back to Albemarle County. The country looked a lot like it had when they moved almost four years ago. There were a few more clearings and cabins now. But gradually the clearings and cabins grew farther apart. By twilight the woods had become dense, and they had not seen a cabin for more than an hour.

George thought, "Ahead is the frontier. Ahead are wilderness and mountains."

They stopped when it got dark. They unsaddled the horses, tethered them where they could reach plenty of grass, and then made camp. They cleaned and roasted the squirrels they had shot along the way.

George and his father were both hungry and ate in silence. Afterward they sat and watched the glowing coals.

George and his father were both hungry and ate in silence. Afterward they sat and watched the glowing coals.

"I like to camp out," George said. "I wish I could camp out all the time."

"Well, it's nice to have a house sometimes," his father said quietly, "especially when the weather's bad."

"I don't mind bad weather," George said. "I could always build a shelter. Or find a cave."

His father stared out into the darkness. His eyes

seemed to look beyond it. "This is still wild country. A strong house can mean a lot."

He sounded serious, and George was silent for a while. Then George said, "Someday I want to ride all over the colonies and sleep out at night. Someday I'm going to be a real woodsman and live in the woods."

His father's face broke into a broad smile. "Fine," he said. "Someday I hope you do. Now let's get some sleep. We want to start early tomorrow."

They slept soundly under their blankets, though the October night was cool. At dawn they rose and made breakfast from the food they had brought in their saddlebags.

George and his father rode two miles before the sun cleared the eastern hills. The woods became denser. About noon Mr. Clark turned off onto a trail that led directly toward the mountains. The place to which they were going was several miles south of the old Clark farm. At dusk they saw the big stone chimney of a cabin on a low hill.

As George and his father rode up the slope, Josiah Lawrence came out. "Ho, there!" He waved. "Welcome! Welcome!"

They rode up to the cabin and dismounted. Mr. Clark and Josiah shook hands heartily.

Then Mr. Lawrence turned to George. "This

doesn't look like the little fellow who went away four years ago, John."

Mr. Clark smiled. "I guess he isn't. He's already talking about becoming a frontiersman."

Mr. Lawrence laughed. He had a loud, roaring laugh. "Good!" he boomed. "We need frontiersmen. There's lots of room for men with wilderness fever."

He jerked his thumb toward the dark line of the Blue Ridge Mountains. "The land beyond those mountains ought to be explored," he went on. "The Indian traders say it's the richest land in the world. Kentucky, the Indians call it. It's a hunter's paradise."

George felt excitement rise. "How old do you have to be to go?"

The two men winked at each other. "Old enough to take care of yourself," Mr. Lawrence said.

George knew they were teasing him. But to himself he thought, "I'll cross those mountains. Sooner than they think."

They ate and went to bed early that night. George and his father were tired from their long ride. George thought the bed felt pretty good. But he didn't think about it long, because he went to sleep almost at once.

Next morning George sat at the breakfast table with his father and Josiah. Mr. Lawrence lived alone and did his own cooking. And he was a good cook.

George started to eat. Then his hand stopped in mid-air. His eyes widened.

A tall, slender Indian boy stood and stared at them from the doorway. He was dressed only in a breechcloth. "Father!" George exclaimed. He had never been so close to an Indian before.

Mr. Lawrence's face broke into a grin. "Come in, Atalpha," he invited.

The young Indian was a little taller than George. He strode to the fireplace and stood quietly.

"My foster son," Mr. Lawrence explained.

Atalpha's eyes narrowed, and he frowned.

"Well, he's not exactly that," Mr. Lawrence said. "I wish he were my son. His people went over into the Kentucky land to hunt. Atalpha was sick with a fever when they left. They knew I would look after him. His family trusts me."

The Indian boy nodded. He didn't smile, but he seemed pleased by this explanation.

"He looks fit as a fiddle now," George's father said.

"Oh, he is," Mr. Lawrence said. "He's hard as nails. And you've never seen a wrestler like him. Best for his age in his tribe."

At the mention of wrestling, George glanced at his father. His eyes flashed.

His father looked doubtful. He knew George was

a good wrestler, but he doubted he could outwrestle an Indian boy.

Mr. Lawrence caught the glint in George's eye. "Are you a wrestler, George?"

"I've done a lot of wrestling with the boys at home," George said.

Atalpha listened with interest. He didn't understand much English, but he knew they were talking about wrestling.

"How would you like to try it with Atalpha here?" Mr. Lawrence asked.

Atalpha said something in his own language. Mr. Lawrence listened, then looked slyly at George. "Atalpha says he can lay the white boy in the dust."

George's face flushed. "I can outwrestle him any day of the. . . ."

"Easy, George," his father interrupted. "You'd better let your actions speak for you. I'd say you'll have your hands full if you wrestle him."

"All right," George said to Mr. Lawrence. "Tell him I'll wrestle him."

"You'll have to tell him yourself," Mr. Lawrence answered. He pointed at the sheathed hunting knife at George's side. "Take your knife outside and stick it in the ground. That's the challenge. If Atalpha steps across the knife it means he accepts the challenge."

George slipped the knife from its sheath. It was an old knife his father had given him. It was dull, and the tip had been broken. But it would still cut small limbs for a fire.

Mr. Lawrence watched George take out the knife, and then he took out his own. He handed it to George. "What do you think of that knife?"

George took Mr. Lawrence's glittering knife. He looked at it with admiration. He touched the long blade very carefully. It was razor sharp.

"It's the best knife I've ever seen," George said.

Mr. Lawrence reached for the knife and slipped it back in its sheath. "I'll tell you what. I'll put my knife up as a stake. The winner will get it, and the sheath, too."

"I've got to win," George thought. That was a real man's knife. He walked outside, and the others followed. Atalpha came last. He smiled. He was sure he could throw George.

George knelt in the clearing and held his own knife high. He looked evenly at Atalpha. The Indian boy stood waiting. His eyes were narrowed and his mouth was set in a grin.

Suddenly George plunged the knife into the earth. Then he jumped quickly to his feet. He stood slightly crouched, waiting for Atalpha to step across the knife. Atalpha came forward. George waited tensely. Atalpha stood in front of the knife.

Then he was across it. He moved so swiftly that George barely had time to step aside as Atalpha lunged. George realized for the first time what he was up against. Atalpha could twist and turn like a cat. He moved as quickly as a cat, too.

George whirled around. The boys approached each other cautiously. They crouched forward on the balls of their feet with knees bent, their arms held slightly forward, ready for an opening. They circled. Each tried to catch the other off balance.

Before George knew what had happened, Atalpha had moved in and locked his arms around George's waist. George felt his breath being squeezed out.

But George wasn't worried. He knew how to break a bear hug. He reached to get a leg behind Atalpha's.

But Atalpha wasn't there. He had twisted and moved magically around behind George. His strong arms squeezed, and George struggled to pull them apart.

Then George's feet were off the ground. His breath was gone and he felt dizzy. In a moment he would be thrown. He couldn't defend himself. His legs kicked wildly.

Then Atalpha hurled George down. George stiff-

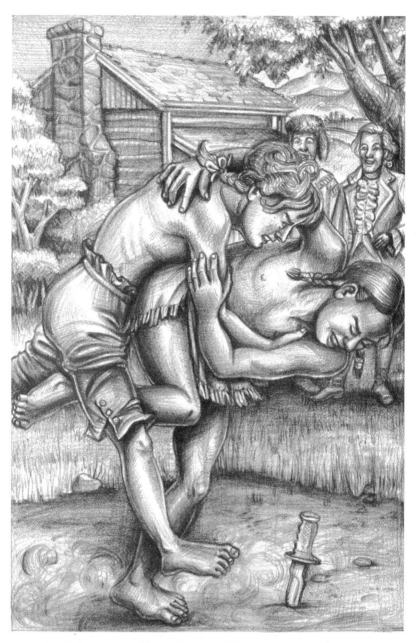

Atalpha was off guard only for a moment, but that
was all George needed.

ened his arms and legs. He crashed down on all fours. Pain shot through his arms and legs, but his body did not touch the ground.

Atalpha felt sure he had thrown George, and he stepped back, panting. He was off guard only for a moment, but that was all George needed. Still on all fours, George sprang sideways. He caught Atalpha with the full force of his body and swung his hips into Atalpha's midsection.

It was a crude move, but effective. Atalpha, relaxed for the moment, went down.

"Good boy, George!" Father yelled. George stood swaying. He was still dizzy. He staggered over and helped Atalpha up.

Atalpha had a puzzled look on his face. He had been sure he would win. Then he held out a hand to George. "Atalpha make mistake," he said. He really spoke better English than George had thought. "White boy smart, catch mistake. White boy fight good."

Mr. Lawrence stepped forward and held out the long, sharp hunting knife. "It's yours, George," he said. "You earned it. I didn't think anyone Atalpha's age could beat him wrestling."

"Well, I was lucky." George Rogers pulled the knife from its sheath. The big blade gleamed in the sunlight. It was a knife worthy of a real woodsman.

Then Atalpha spoke in his Indian tongue. Mr. Lawrence listened and translated for the Clarks. "Atalpha says the trappers beyond the mountains— he means in Kentucky carry big knives. His people call the trappers Big Knives."

Atalpha nodded. He pointed at George. "You— Big Knife."

"That's a compliment, George," Mr. Lawrence said. "I guess that makes you a real frontiersman."

George slipped the knife into its sheath and put the sheath on his belt. He felt a foot taller. Then he remembered his uneaten breakfast still on the table inside. He grinned at Atalpha. "Big Knife hungry," he said, pointing at the house. "Eat breakfast."

Chapter 5

First Deer

George's father came in the front door. He walked to the fire and warmed his hands. It was a bright day, but outside the air was brisk and cold. It had been more than a month since the trip to Albemarle County.

"Where were you, John?" Mother asked.

Mr. Clark rubbed his bands together. "I went out to the springhouse to check the meat supply. We're getting low."

George was cleaning the Deckard. His father let him clean the long rifle, and had explained the correct way to fire it. George had practiced holding it and pulling the trigger.

"George," his father said, "I think it's about time you got yourself a deer."

George felt like leaping on the table and yelling for joy. But he only grinned widely and remained quiet. His father said a real man had self-control.

"It's still early," his father went on. "We'll start right away. Hurry and put your hunting clothes on, George."

George was already on his way upstairs to change. When he came down he had his bow and arrows, and the hunting knife he had won was strapped to his side.

"Leave your bow here," his father said. "But bring the knife. We'll need it."

George and his father stalked through the woods. They went down gullies and up slopes, across clearings and around thickets. The deer were like invisible and silent ghosts. They saw only squirrels and birds and an occasional rabbit that morning.

George was glad now that he didn't have his bow and arrows. Even his father was beginning to tire from carrying the Deckard all morning and afternoon.

"There," his father said suddenly, pointing. "Fresh tracks."

"At last!" George started off in the direction the tracks went.

"Wait," his father cautioned. He picked up a handful of leaves and let them fall slowly through his fingers. The wind carried them away in brilliant swirls. "You see?" he said. "The wind is behind us. If we come up from this direction the deer will catch our scent."

"Oh," said George. "I forgot." Hunting deer wasn't like hunting squirrels.

"We'll swing around in a circle and try to get downwind of the deer," his father said. He started out at a right angle to the way George had started. George followed, copying the silent, careful tread of his father.

They went quietly for some distance. They came to the creek below a sharp bend where the current had washed out a wide pool. Animals went there to drink. George's father primed the gun. He turned to George and put a finger to his lips. Then he started slowly and quietly along the edge of the creek, toward the bend.

George followed excitedly. He knew what his father was thinking. The deer would probably be drinking at the pool. They were almost to the bend when a rabbit hopped out of some brush. George jumped, and a twig snapped beneath his foot. His father motioned George to be quiet.

Then George gasped. A deer lifted its head from drinking and sniffed the air. It was a beautiful stag, about thirty-five yards ahead of them.

"Take your time," his father whispered. He

pulled back the clumsy hammer of the Deckard and shoved the rifle into George's hands.

George could hardly see because his heart was beating so hard. His whole body seemed to shake with excitement.

Father nodded. "Go ahead."

George raised the powerful gun with trembling arms. He had fired the Deckard twice before, at a target. It had a bone-crushing kick, and he'd had a bruise for a week.

The deer hadn't scented them, but it seemed to sense danger. It stood alert and then began to move forward slowly, away from the pool.

George sighted down the long barrel. The deer swam before his eyes. It was coming closer and closer. It looked as big as a horse.

"Shoot!" his father hissed.

George's finger was tight on the trigger. He tried to remember everything his father had told him about shooting. He wanted to squeeze the shot off, but how could you shoot an animal that big? Squirrels, small animals, were different. He'd never realized how large a deer was.

Then he jerked the trigger. The gun went off with a roar. George knew he had done it all wrong. He had shut both eyes tight. And he hadn't squeezed the trigger. He'd jerked it.

George raised the powerful gun with trembling arms.

The Deckard's kick almost knocked him over backward. His shoulder ached where the rifle butt rammed it. He opened his eyes slowly. The last wisps of gunpowder smoke were trailing off in the breeze, but the burnt-powder smell still hung in the air. The deer had already disappeared.

"I missed," George said.

His father smiled. "That's all right. There aren't many boys who hit a deer on their first try."

"But they're so big!" George exclaimed. "How could I miss?"

"I guess that's part of the trouble," his father said with a grin.

Then George knew his father understood. There was something different about killing an animal that big. There was a thrill in it, but something frightening, too.

"I think I was scared of the kick," George said. "I did everything wrong."

"You'll be ready next time," his father said. "It's not like shooting a squirrel, though, is it?" George nodded in agreement.

The next day was as sunny as the one before, but warmer. "A perfect day," George's mother said at breakfast.

"A perfect day to get a deer," said his father.

George stuffed the last bit of buckwheat cake in his mouth. He stood up and drained the rest of the milk from his mug. Then he rushed in and got the Deckard. He had cleaned it spotless last night, but he wanted to clean it again before they went out.

"Today I'll do everything right," George thought. "Today I'll get my first deer."

He didn't have to wait long. He and his father found fresh tracks before they had been hunting an hour.

They came on the deer before they expected to, nibbling the grass in a clearing. It was smaller than the one yesterday, but it was still a good deer.

His father hastily primed the gun and cocked

the hammer. He had intended to let George do it, but there wasn't time. He shoved the long rifle into George's hands. The deer caught their scent and raised his head in alarm.

"Quick," his father whispered. "He smells us."

George's hands trembled. He took a deep breath and let it out until he felt relaxed. He squeezed steadily on the trigger. His eye held the deer in the gun sight.

The deer tensed and turned to bound away. The gun thundered through the quiet woods.

"You got him!" his father exclaimed.

The deer took one step after the shot and then fell heavily. George and his father hurried toward it. As they got near to the animal, his father suddenly put out a hand. "Wait," he said.

He took George's hunting knife. He went to the deer and knelt cautiously beside it. Then he plunged the knife into the deer's neck. He beckoned to George.

"You have to be careful with deer," his father said. "Sometimes they look dead, but aren't. I've seen a wounded deer get up and attack a careless hunter. Those antlers can do a lot of damage if you give them a chance."

George knelt by the deer. He felt the strong, hard antlers. A thin trickle of blood ran down just behind the front shoulder. It had been a perfect shot.

He ran his hand across the proud head. "It isn't exactly the way I thought it would be," George said. "To kill a deer, I mean. I feel kind of sick."

His father's face was serious, and his eyes were bright. "I think you'll make a fine woodsman, George," he said. "You have respect for life. I hope you'll always have that respect."

George wiped his hunting knife in the leaves and slipped it back in the sheath. Next time he would use the knife himself. And he would handle the gun by himself, too. He had a name to live up to—Big Knife.

George looked down at the deer and then up at his father. "But I did it right this time, didn't I?" he said.

Chapter 6

A Night in the Woods

George walked briskly along the ridge above the creek, carrying a new rifle. He and Jonathan shared one their father had bought. The leather sheath of the knife he had won a year ago was fastened to his belt. Rex, his hound, ran ahead of him.

George was hunting squirrels. Though he didn't really need the dog, Rex always went along. If he spied a squirrel, he gave a little whine. But he didn't move or bark. With his father's help, George had trained him well. "That dog's almost human," his father often said.

George walked lightly and carefully. He kept his eyes moving, watching the trees. He didn't mind not seeing any squirrels. Just being out in the brisk October air was enough.

The shadows were starting to lengthen before George realized how late it was. He looked to the west. The sun was a red ball through the trees. "We'd better head back," he said to Rex.

Their neighbor Mr. Strong had ridden over to the Clark home yesterday. He told them that a panther had been seen in the woods the day before. George knew it wouldn't be wise to stay in the woods after dark. The panther probably wouldn't attack a man unless it was attacked first, but it was safest not to count on it.

Rex was sniffing along the ground. Suddenly he barked and set out at a run. George knew he really should start back home. But Rex might have picked up a raccoon or possum trail.

George decided to follow for a little way. If he didn't find something soon, he'd call Rex off.

Rex had disappeared into the thickets along the creek. George could hear him baying. A few moments later the dog appeared on the opposite slope, running fast.

George rushed down to the creek. He waded across and started up the sloping trail to High Point. He could hear Rex baying farther up the hill. High Point was the tallest, steepest hill around. From the top of it the stream looked like a small, bright string.

Then Rex's baying changed. George listened intently. He had never heard his dog make sounds like these before. These were sharp, piercing yelps.

Suddenly a chill ran up George's spine. He knew why the cries were different. They were cries of pain.

George flew up the steep hill. As he approached the top, he could hear whines off to the right of the trail. He plunged into the woods.

Briers caught at his clothes, and low-hanging limbs scraped his face. Vines wrapped themselves around his body. Roots almost sent him sprawling. But he struggled on.

George could hear Rex whimpering close by. He pulled himself up against a huge dead tree. Then he saw Rex.

The hound lay under a big rotten limb. Years ago lightning had struck the tree and nearly splintered it in half. Then the tree had died and the wood had rotted. Now the wind had broken one of the limbs and it had crashed to the ground on top of Rex.

George rushed forward. The light end of the limb lay across Rex's hind legs. If the heavy end of the limb had caught him, he would surely have been killed.

George struggled with the mass of rotten wood. He lifted and shoved. The limb moved slowly, and then it was off. Rex whined and tried to get to his feet. But his back legs didn't move.

Rex lay under a big rotten limb.

George made the dog lie down. There was some blood on the ground. "Stay there, boy," he said. He stroked the dog soothingly.

George stood up and looked around. What could he do? "I guess I'll have to carry you," he said.

Rex was full-grown now and weighed more than twenty pounds. George gathered Rex into his arms with difficulty. He had to be careful because the dog's legs might be broken.

He started toward the path. Rex was much heavier than he had thought. It took all his strength to carry the dog and at the same time make his way through the trees.

Soon he had to stop. He placed Rex gently on the ground. The dog whined. George stood panting. He wished there were something he could do to ease the dog's pain. "I'll just have to get you home," he said.

He stooped and lifted the dog again. This time he kept on until he just had to stop. The afternoon in the woods and his struggle with the heavy limb had tired him. He couldn't go on.

He squinted through the trees. There was a dim glow in the western sky, but the sun was gone. It would soon be dark.

"This is awful," George said. The hound whimpered and looked up with trusting eyes. "You can't walk, and I can't carry you." Rex whimpered again. "Don't worry, boy," George said. "I won't leave you."

He petted the dog. Then he started to gather firewood. If they were going to be in the woods after dark, they'd need a fire. He remembered the panther and looked around for his gun. It wasn't there! He groaned. He'd leaned it against the tree when he found Rex. He felt for his knife at his side.

It was too late to go back for the gun. He might lose his way in the dark. Anyway, he couldn't leave Rex alone, and a fire should keep the panther away.

But if worst came to worst he still had his knife.

George built a wind shelter with some of the larger branches he found. Then he cleared away some leaves on the ground and laid short pieces of wood in a circle. He used his knife to cut shavings onto a small pile of dead leaves inside the circle. He took out his flint box and struck sparks over the dry shavings and leaves.

A tiny flame shot up quickly. George cupped his hands around it and blew gently on the shavings. As they burned, he added small twigs, and when they began to burn he added larger twigs. Finally he was able to add thick limbs broken into short pieces. The dry wood made a smokeless fire with bright, clear flames.

Exhausted, George sat with Rex's head on his lap. The dog was able to move his legs a little now, but he still couldn't stand. George's hopes rose. Perhaps the injury wasn't as bad as he had thought. He petted the dog and Rex nuzzled his hand. The fire grew brighter and hotter.

George watched the moon rise over a bank of clouds. He took a branch from the pile of wood beside him and threw it into the fire. Sparks flew upward. George rubbed Rex behind the ears. "We're all right," he said comfortingly.

A sound in the brush beyond the circle of fire-

George sat motionless, listening harder than he
had ever listened in his life.

light sent chills of fear through him. He slipped the hunting knife from its sheath. Rex bared his teeth and growled without raising his head.

George sat motionless, listening harder than he had ever listened in his life. But he heard only the fire and the wind rustling the leaves.

At last he relaxed and slipped his knife back in its sheath. If only he hadn't forgotten his gun! When he grew up and went to Kentucky, he couldn't make a mistake like forgetting his rifle. "And Kentucky's where I'm going," he said aloud.

The fire burned higher, sending out more warmth. George leaned back against the shelter and closed his eyes for a moment. Then he slept.

From a long way off he heard someone call, "George Rogers!" He opened his eyes and saw the moon high in the sky.

"Wake up, son." George's father and York were standing over him. His father held a flaming pine knot.

George rubbed his eyes. "Hello," he said. "I'm glad you came. How did you find us?"

"We knew something was wrong when you didn't come home," his father started to explain.

"Wait." George reached down and petted Rex's head. Rex whined. "Rex got hurt," George said. "Part of an old tree fell on him, and I'm afraid his legs are broken. I tried to carry him, but I couldn't. He's too heavy."

Father bent and held the pine knot above the dog. He felt his legs carefully. "I think he'll be all right," he said finally. "I can't be sure, though. We can tell better when we get him home."

"I'll carry him," York said. "I'll be mighty careful with him."

"Here's your gun." His father held out George's rifle.

George was surprised. "How did you find it?"

"We found the spot where the tree limb fell," his father answered. "Your rifle was propped against the trunk. When we saw the blood we were afraid you had been hurt."

"No, I'm all right," George said. "But it was a bad mistake to leave my gun like that. Especially with that panther around. I heard him move around in the brush once."

"That's funny," his father said. "Mr. Strong came over this evening and said he'd killed it."

George was very quiet as they broke through the woods, his father leading the way with the flaming pine knot. When they had found the trail and were on the way home George said, "You know, I'm glad it wasn't really a panther."

Chapter 7

The Student

George Rogers looked out the window and thought about hunting, tracking and camping—the things he used to do at home.

"Is your exercise copied?" The schoolmaster's voice broke in on his thoughts.

George jumped. Quickly he handed Mr. Robertson his copybook with its half-finished page of writing. Mr. Robertson took it and pushed his spectacles up on his forehead. Sometimes his nephew George provoked him.

George and Jonathan had gone to study at the Reverend Donald Robertson's little school in Dunkirk. They stayed with Grandfather Rogers, whose plantation was nearby. George didn't like school very much. He couldn't keep his mind on schoolwork.

Mr. Robertson handed the copybook back to

George. "George Rogers," he said, "I know you have a brain. Will you never use it?"

"I—I try, sir," George answered.

"Name the rulers of England," Mr. Robertson commanded.

George thought. Mr. Robertson tapped his fingers impatiently on the desk top. Then he named the first kings, in order to hurry George along. "Alfred the Great, Edward. . . ."

George had studied England's rulers last night. He began to remember. "Athelstane, the Six Boy Kings. . ." He hesitated. He couldn't remember any more. There was a long silence. He sighed. "It's no use."

"Have you studied them?"

"Yes, sir," George answered. "But I just can't remember them."

"James Madison, let me hear you name them."

The slender, fair-haired boy in the next seat stood and glanced at George Rogers.

"Well?" Mr. Robertson asked sharply.

"Alfred," James Madison began. "Edward, Athelstane, the Six Boy Kings, Canute, Harold Harefoot, Hardicanute. . ."

George stared straight ahead. His thoughts wandered again and he hardly heard the names as James recited them. He remembered how his dog,

Rex, had gone out in the woods with him, even before his back legs were completely well. Rex had limped along, eager as ever.

That had been a little over a year ago, but it seemed a lot longer.

"William, Anne, George the First, George the Second, George the Third," James finished.

"Splendid!" Mr. Robertson exclaimed. He walked to the front of the room and closed the book on his desk. "Dismissed," he said.

George's long legs carried him so swiftly that he was among the first to shove his way outside. He was always one of the first.

In the yard George flopped down under a tree to wait for Jonathan. He felt better now that school was out for the day. But his books lying on the ground reminded him that he had lessons to prepare over the weekend, and list after list of things to memorize.

Jonathan came over with Jemmy Madison. Jemmy said, "I hated to answer that question when you couldn't, George."

"That's all right," George said. "You're a good student. I'm not, that's all."

"Have you studied your Latin for that examination on Monday?" Jonathan asked Jemmy.

"No, I was going to do it tomorrow."

Jonathan came over with Jemmy Madison.

George's face brightened. "Can you come over to Grandfather's tomorrow?"

"I guess so," Jemmy replied. "Do you want to study Latin?"

"Well, not really," George said. "But maybe you can help me learn that vocabulary list."

"Come on," Jonathan urged. "It's getting late, George. We'd better go."

George gathered up his books. Then he and Jonathan started off to get the horses they rode to school, in the stables down at the other end of the street. "See you tomorrow," Jemmy said. George and Jonathan waved goodbye.

When they got home, George could hear his grandfather talking to someone in the sitting room. He started to pass the sitting room door. Then he pulled up short. His grandfather and Mr. Robertson were looking straight at him.

"Come in, boy," his grandfather said.

George entered the room. He felt worried.

"We were just talking about you, George," Mr. Robertson said.

George swallowed hard. He had been afraid of that. No doubt Uncle Donald had said a lot about his schoolwork.

"Your uncle tells me you don't seem very happy in school," his grandfather said.

George couldn't think of anything to say. How could he explain? His grandfather might understand, but he didn't think Uncle Donald would.

"I understand you are interested in going over the mountains," Mr. Robertson said.

"Yes, sir," George replied.

"There are many things you should know if you want to go into strange country."

"Yes, sir."

His grandfather said, "That's true. That's true. You ought to know surveying, for one thing. New country must be mapped out."

"That's right," Mr. Robertson said. "A man has to teach himself a great many things. Sometimes it's difficult, but it has to be done if a man wants to succeed."

George thought he saw a smile pass between his grandfather and his uncle.

That night George studied by the fire while his grandfather dozed in his chair. Jonathan had already finished his lessons and had gone to bed.

At last George pushed the book away from him in disgust. "I can't learn these lists of Latin words," he muttered.

"That's because you don't think they are important," his grandfather said.

"I thought you were asleep. . . ."

His grandfather chuckled. "I've been watching you for a half hour. You've been as cross and grumpy as an old setting hen."

George ran a hand through his rumpled hair. "I know I have. I hope Jemmy has better luck teaching me than Jonathan had. This is harder work than plowing a cornfield. And I don't like to plow, either."

"What do you like?" his grandfather asked.

"Not school, that's for sure."

The old man smiled. "They say my father—your great-grandfather Giles—was like that. Maybe you're a chip off the old block."

"Sometimes I think I'm not like anybody else in the world," George said in a discouraged voice. "Jonathan likes to farm. I don't. Uncle George's boys like to work in his mill. I don't. And I'm no good at school."

"What do you really like to do?" his grandfather asked again.

George was sitting on the floor with his knees drawn up under his chin. His face brightened. "I like to hunt, fish, swim, wrestle and just wander through the woods. And I like people, but I don't mind being alone. I never feel lonely in the woods. There are too many things to see and think about."

"Such as?"

His grandfather gave an understanding smile. "Now I know you have a bit of your great-grandfather Giles in you."

"There are always animal tracks to follow," George explained. "And I like to hunt, though some people think it is hard work."

His grandfather gave an understanding smile. "Now I know you have a bit of your great-grandfather Giles in you. He was always a wilderness man at heart. But he stayed near the Tidewater so that we could go to school."

"All of Virginia was a wilderness in those days, wasn't it?" George asked.

His grandfather nodded. "I made my living as a surveyor when I was young."

George suddenly sat up very straight. "Maybe I could be a surveyor. You said that I ought to know surveying. I might be good at it!"

The old man raised his eyebrows.

"Why couldn't I be?" George asked eagerly.

His grandfather's eyes twinkled. "Maybe you'd make a good one. Your Uncle Donald says you will never make a scholar."

George nodded. He felt a little ashamed, but he knew that what his uncle said was true.

"I have the feeling that most of your schooling will be from the book of nature—nature itself."

"That's it!" George exclaimed. "I knew you understood, Grandfather."

"I've thought about you a good deal, my boy. By the laws of Virginia, Jonathan will inherit your father's plantation."

"I don't want it," George said with spirit. "I don't want to be tied down to a farm. I want to be free to go over the mountains."

His grandfather nodded again. "That's why I've

decided to give you all my surveying instruments. You can learn to be a surveyor."

George could hardly believe his ears. He knew that his grandfather prized those instruments—the tripod and sighting device and other things—but he didn't know how they were used.

"And starting Monday you'll have a teacher—me—to show you how to use them," his grandfather said. "You know, you always need a teacher to help you."

"Yes, sir!" George said happily.

"You'll have to pay attention to my lessons," his grandfather told him. "I told your Uncle Donald I'd make you study hard."

"I will," George promised. Now he understood why his grandfather and this uncle had smiled at each other this afternoon.

His grandfather's face was as mischievous as a boy's. "I thought I would save this surprise for you until Jemmy came over tomorrow. But now you can tell him yourself."

George scarcely heard his grandfather's last words. He was thinking hard about the future. "I'll need surveying when I go West. I intend to go as soon as I can."

"The West is a bonny land, they say," the old man told him. "I wish I was young enough to go with you. But my old bones are too brittle."

"I wish I could start tomorrow," George said wistfully.

"In the meantime, we'll start our surveying lessons on Monday," his grandfather said dryly.

George laughed. "That will be one school where I'm sure I'll be a first-rate scholar!"

Chapter 8

A Visit to Williamsburg

The horses kicked up dust from Duke of Gloucester Street. George and Jonathan were home for the summer, and their father had sent them to Williamsburg to deliver a letter.

Ten years had passed since the day in 1757 when the Clarks had made the journey from Albemarle County back to the Tidewater. George was thinking about that trip as he and Jonathan rode through the Virginia capital.

George remembered saying goodbye to a red-headed boy named Tom Jefferson. Though they had promised to visit, they had not seen each other since that day. George had heard that Tom was in Williamsburg this summer, and hoped he would get a chance to see him.

Father had warned him that Tom would be changed. George was fourteen now, and Tom was older than George. Tom was practically a lawyer.

He'd been studying for years. George wondered if Tom might have forgotten him.

George had changed a lot, too. He had grown into a tall, strong young man. Grandfather said he was almost a finished surveyor. George had worked hard.

George and Jonathan let their horses move at a slow walk down the street. It had been a long ride to Williamsburg, and the horses were tired. Suddenly George reined his horse to a stop.

"Come on," Jonathan said. "Let's get this letter delivered. Then we can take a rest."

But George didn't answer. He was staring ahead of them at a young man walking briskly along the path.

Jonathan turned to look.

"Do you know who that is?" George exclaimed.

Jonathan looked closely. "It's nobody I know."

"Oh, yes, it is," George answered. He headed his horse toward the young man.

As George rode up to him, the man stopped and gave him a puzzled look. "Yes?" he said. "Did you want to see me?"

George said nothing. This was certainly Tom Jefferson, but it looked as if Tom didn't remember him at all. He hadn't really thought Tom would forget.

The young man stared at George. "What is it you want?"

George reached up and jerked off his cap. His red hair gleamed in the sunlight.

The young man's eyes narrowed. Then his expression turned to one of delighted surprise. "George Rogers Clark!"

George leaped down from his horse. Tom Jefferson took his hand and shook it soundly. "What a surprise!" Tom said. He stared at George as if he could hardly believe his eyes.

By this time Jonathan had ridden up to the pair. Tom glanced up and recognized him. "And Jonathan! What in the world are you two doing in Williamsburg?"

"We have to deliver a letter," George said.

"I just can't believe it," Tom said. "It's been years. I didn't even recognize you."

"You recognized this, though," George said, and he pointed to his hair.

Tom laughed. "Yes, I'd know that red hair anywhere."

"I'm not sure I'd have recognized you with a hat on," George said.

"Well, I'm glad I didn't wear my hat," Tom replied. "Did you two just arrive?"

Jonathan nodded. "We'll stay overnight and ride back in the morning."

"Good," Tom said. "Then we'll have time for a real visit."

"What a surprise!" Tom said. He stared at George as if he could hardly believe his eyes.

"First we have to deliver Father's letter to the Clerk of the House of Burgesses," George said.

"Do you know where you're going to stay?" Tom asked.

"No," Jonathan answered. "Father said there were inns."

"Yes," Tom said. "There's a good one just down

the street. I'll go with you. I hope you can get a room—the town's crowded now."

Jonathan got off his horse. The three of them walked together down the dusty street, with George and Jonathan leading their horses.

They got a room at the inn, and then Tom took them over to the House of Burgesses to deliver the letter. After that they stopped by the stables to board the horses for the night.

Back at the inn, Tom led them to a wooden table near a window. He asked the innkeeper for three meat pies.

"So even your father is writing to the House of Burgesses," Tom said after their food had been brought. "Many people write to the Burgesses these days to petition for something."

A sandy-haired young man came in and went to a table at which three other men were already seated. He waved and smiled broadly at Tom Jefferson as he passed.

"Who's that?" George asked.

"His name is Patrick Henry," Tom replied. "He's a popular fellow around here." Then he smiled. "Though I'm afraid he's not very popular with the King's crowd. In fact, none of my friends are."

Jonathan's face lit up. "He's the one who introduced the resolution against the Stamp Act two years ago, isn't he?"

George tried to remember what the Stamp Act was. The King had ordered that all legal papers in the colonies be written on paper bearing an English stamp. And the King had then charged the Colonials very high fees for the stamps.

"That was a grand speech he made in the House of Burgesses," Jonathan said.

"Yes," Tom grinned. "Patrick Henry isn't a man to mince words."

Tom turned and looked at George for a few moments. At last he shook his head. "Well, George Rogers Clark." He smiled and seemed to be remembering something. "Are you still the fisherman you used to be?"

"Yes," George answered, "but I've taken to hunting more than fishing."

"What are you doing now?" Tom asked.

"I've been studying surveying," George answered. "Jonathan's in school at Dunkirk."

"Well, there's a lot of country to be surveyed," Tom said.

"Are you still in college?" Jonathan asked.

"No, I've finished college," Tom said. "And I've just finished studying law with one of the best lawyers in Virginia. He introduced me to Patrick Henry."

"I'd like to meet him," Jonathan said.

"I think that can be arranged," Tom said. "You must be interested in politics. I am too."

"I do fairly well in history," Jonathan said. "But I don't think I'd be a good politician. Plantation life is just right for me."

"What do you plan to do, George?" Tom asked. He clapped George on the shoulder.

"Well, after this summer I'll study surveying some more," George replied.

"No," Tom said. "I mean what will you do later on? Will you help your father run the plantation, or will you be a surveyor?"

"I'll go into Kentucky territory," George said.

"That's dangerous country," Tom said. "But then, you never could stay out of the woods, even when you were five." He grinned.

George smiled back, but he felt uncomfortable. No one seemed to take him seriously when he talked about the wilderness. He had been sure Tom Jefferson would understand.

Just then Patrick Henry walked past their table. Tom stopped him and introduced him to George and Jonathan.

When he had gone they talked about other things. They talked all through the evening and late into the night.

At last Tom got up and said they'd better be getting to bed. He had to get up early in the morning and so did they.

When he left them at the inn he said, "I'll meet you at the stables at seven and see you off."

Next morning George and Jonathan had just led their horses out of the stables when Tom appeared. He strode briskly in the cool morning air.

"Sleep well?" he asked.

"Fine," George answered.

Jonathan nodded.

"Well, give your folks my regards," Tom said. "And tell them I'm sorry I never got around to making that visit."

George and Jonathan mounted their horses. Tom looked up at George.

His face was serious. "George," he said, "I'm glad to have seen you again. If you get a chance to send me a letter, I wish you would. If I can, I'll write, too. There's a lot of wilderness around, and I have a feeling no one will be able to keep you out of it. So be careful, but go ahead. You must do what you think is important to you."

Suddenly George knew that Tom Jefferson was the best friend he'd ever had. Ten years hadn't changed that. "Thanks, Tom," he said. He leaned down to shake hands. "Goodbye."

Jonathan rode up beside him. "Goodbye, Tom," he said.

They turned their horses and rode away, making small puffs of dust along the street.

George turned to wave once more. Tom Jefferson stood just in front of the eight-sided gunpowder storehouse. His red hair flashed as he waved back.

Chapter 9

Flash Flood

On a morning in the spring of 1771, George Rogers Clark woke to the sound of rain pounding on the roof. He stretched and squinted at the window. The rain meant no work today.

His father had left George in charge of the plantation. He and Jonathan had gone on a business trip to Richmond. George was eighteen now, and had a man's responsibilities.

John hurried into George's room. "Are you going to sleep all day?" he teased.

George playfully threw a pillow at his younger brother. "What else is there to do on a rainy day like this?"

"I thought you were going to show me some more about surveying," John complained.

"You want me to show you how to survey mud?" George laughed.

"Well, the children are cross and noisy because they can't go outside," John said. "Ann wants you to come and help her quiet them."

The Clark family had grown larger since they had moved back to Caroline County. George had three new brothers and two new sisters.

Today, their mother would return from her visit to Aunt Rachel Rogers. William, the newest son, was with her. He was just eight months old.

George dressed and hurried downstairs with John. Ann did look upset. A wisp of hair hung in front of her eyes. She blew it back.

"For goodness' sake, help me get the children quieted down," Ann said to George.

The sounds of children yelling and running seemed to rise from all over the house. "Why didn't you get John to help you?" George asked. "What's he doing?"

"That John is as bad as the rest of them," she said. "A fourteen-year-old boy ought to have more responsibility."

"I'll have more responsibility when George takes me West with him," John said.

George smiled. "Don't let Mother hear you say that. She'd give me a good tongue-lashing if she thought I encouraged you to go."

Ann sighed. "I'll be glad when Mother gets back.

She'll settle these ruffians in a hurry."

"Well, let's get them rounded up," George said. "Maybe we can teach them a game."

Ann, George, and John set off in different directions, and met again in the sitting room.

"You mean Elizabeth and Lucy were making all that noise?" George asked in amazement.

Ann held three-year-old Elizabeth, and John was hanging on to four-year-old Lucy.

"That's right," John said.

"Where are Richard and Edmund?"

"Oh, they went out early this morning to play on the island in the creek," Ann replied.

"In this rain?" George was alarmed.

"It wasn't raining when they left," Ann said.

George frowned and looked at his younger brother. "John, you should've called them in when the rain began. A heavy rain like this could cause a sudden flood in the creek."

"I didn't think about that, George," John said.

George put on his coat and rushed out the door. It really was a downpour. Lightning flashed across the sky and thunder rolled. A strong wind had come up, and tall trees were bent halfway to the ground.

He rushed to the stable. There was no time to

saddle a horse, so he slipped a bridle over the head of a fast roan, jumped on the horse's back, and raced toward the creek.

Wind tore at his clothes and rain peppered his face like needles. George slipped first to one side and then the other on the horse's wet back.

At last he reached the steep hill that overlooked the island in the creek. He urged the horse up the muddy slope, but the wind and rain and mud were too much for the animal.

George leapt from the horse's back and went up the rest of the hill on foot. He reached the top and peered down through the blinding rain. The island was right below him.

Richard and Edmund were waist-deep in the muddy, swirling water, clinging to the small trees that grew on the island. George had made it just in time.

George pulled off his heavy leather boots, slid down the muddy hillside, and plunged into the water. It came to his waist and it was rising fast.

The current knocked his feet from under him.

He got up again and struggled toward the island. Although the water knocked him off balance several times, he reached the island at last.

There was no time to lose. George yelled above the roar of the storm and water, "Hang on to me!"

Richard and Edmund were waist-deep in the
muddy, swirling water, clinging to the small
trees that grew on the island.

He reached out to his terrified little brothers.

Richard climbed on George's back and clung des-
perately to his neck. George picked up Edmund and
lifted him on his shoulders. Edmund held fast to
George's hair. It hurt like anything.

As George started back to the bank, the water
was up to his chest. The weight of his brothers and

the current kept pulling him down, but he managed to stumble toward the bank.

Finally he reached it. He grabbed at large roots which stuck out where the water had washed the bank away. He was able to hold the three of them there, but he couldn't climb up because of the mud. The water was rising faster, and roared past them with great force.

Then George heard a voice above the wind. "George!" He looked up and saw John at the top of the steep hill.

Now something swished past George's head. He saw a loop of rope dangling beside him. John had been smart enough to know they would need a rope.

George yelled, "Hang on!" and let go of Edmund. Edmund clung tighter than ever to George's hair. Richard's arms stayed wrapped around George's neck.

George reached up and grabbed the loop of rope. He dropped it over Edmund's head. Then he put the loop under his arms and pulled the slipknot tight. He gave the rope a tug.

John began to pull Edmund up. He got him to the top and slipped the rope off. Then he dropped the loop again.

George grabbed it and slipped the rope over Richard's shoulders. When he had pulled the knot tight, he tugged. John pulled Richard up.

George could no longer touch the bottom of the creek bed. His body was swept away from the bank, but he clung tightly to the roots.

When the rope sailed down again, George caught it with one hand and then the other. He was drawn slowly up the long muddy incline.

At the top he sat in the mud. The rain still fell in torrents. Edmund and Richard were sobbing at the top of their lungs.

George looked up at John.

"I was afraid I'd be too late," John said.

"You were right on time," George answered.

"It took a lot of courage to do what you did," John said.

George grinned. "It took a rope, too."

John grinned back. Then they picked up Richard and Edmund and started back home.

Their mother got home late that afternoon with baby William. She was shocked to see that a chimney had been blown down, but relieved when she saw that everyone was safe and sound.

The little girls were taking their naps. Richard and Edmund were playing a game in front of the fire, and Ann was sewing.

"My, wasn't that a storm!" their mother said.

"Yes," Ann replied. "It blew a chimney over."

"So I saw," their mother said.

George and Jonathan came in. "What have you two been up to?" she asked.

"Oh, nothing, Mother," George replied. "Nothing at all."

"Well, if you have nothing to do, why don't you see about getting that chimney fixed?"

George stretched and yawned. Then he grinned at John. "Come on," he said. "Let's go take a look at that chimney."

The two brothers walked to the door. As they went out George threw an arm over John's shoulder. "John," he said, "I think I'll start out for the West one of these days soon. Maybe I'll take little William with me."

Mother frowned. She didn't like him to joke about going West. She believed that only a foolish person would go there in these dangerous times.

"It's so dull around here," George said to John with a sigh. "Nothing ever happens."

George soon did leave for the West. He crossed the Allegheny Mountains, and traveled down the Ohio River. In the summer of 1772, he returned and told his family about his travels. Where the Kanawha river flows into the Ohio, he had surveyed some land and laid out a claim, and he promised to do the same for his father. He joked

George soon did leave for the West.

that he'd leave some for his littlest brother, William Clark, then two years old. Thirty years later, William headed West too, very far West, with the family's slave, York, as one of the two leaders of the Lewis and Clark expedition to explore the Louisiana Territory.

Chapter 10

Fifty Years Later

A grandfather sat by the fire in Lexington, Kentucky. His grandchildren Betty Lou and Jerry sat in front of him. "Would you like me to tell a story?" Grandfather asked.

They both nodded.

"Do you know who George Rogers Clark was?" Grandfather asked.

Betty Lou shook her head. Jerry thought. He had heard that name in school. "He and Meriwether Lewis were the first men to go clear across the West to Oregon," he said.

The old gentleman shook his head. "You're mixed up." He smiled. "But then a lot of people get his name mixed up. No, that was George's younger brother, Will Clark. Will was a great man, too. But George Rogers is the one I want to tell you about."

Jerry looked up at the long, shining sword that hung over the mantel. "Did you use that when you were with George Rogers Clark?"

"No," Grandfather answered. "I used that sword in the War of 1812. But I'm thinking of a time long ago when I fought under George Rogers Clark. He was the best and bravest soldier I've ever known.

"In 1778 the Americans were fighting the Revolutionary War. George Rogers Clark was only twenty-six. There were older and more famous men in Kentucky. But the settlers chose Clark to defend them. He had a wise head on young shoulders. He had tremendous energy and spirit. And he knew the wilderness.

"Indians were attacking the settlements in Kentucky. Clark realized the Indians would attack the Kentuckians as long as they could get guns and powder. Hamilton, the British lieutenant governor at Detroit, kept them supplied through the British forts. We called Hamilton 'the Hair-buyer' because he paid the Indians money for American scalps.

"Young Clark knew that if he could capture the British forts in the Northwest, he could turn the tables. But that was a mighty big order.

"The French had surrendered their forts to the British some twenty years before. Most of the people in the towns were still French. Now the King of France had become an ally, a friend, of the Americans. So Clark counted on the French in the

Northwest to help him."

"Did they?" Jerry asked.

"Now wait," Grandfather said. "I don't want to get ahead of my story. Clark went back to Virginia, where he had grown up. He went to see Governor Patrick Henry and presented his plan. His old friend, Thomas Jefferson, supported him. Governor Henry gave him supplies and ammunition and said he could enlist soldiers. But Clark couldn't get half the men he wanted. Many thought his plan too risky.

"Clark and his small band floated down the river till they came to the falls of the Ohio—at Louisville, you know. That's where I enlisted. I was just a youngster, but I had heard so much about Clark that I would have followed him anywhere.

"We went on down the river, landed on the north bank of the Ohio, and marched west across the Illinois country. Talk about surprising the enemy! The British were so surprised they surrendered their fort at Kaskaskia without firing a shot.

"The other forts fell just as easily. Clark even sent a small force back east to Vincennes on the Wabash River, and the fort there gave up, too. Everywhere we went the French welcomed us. And Clark knew how to handle the Indians. He was a diplomat as well as a soldier.

"Well, when Hamilton heard what had happened, he flew into a rage. He was more upset about Vincennes than anything else. That was a most important fort.

"Now imagine that it is the end of January in the year 1779. A rider comes to the fort at Kaskaskia. He enters the fort and rushes to see the commander. The commander, of course, is Colonel George Rogers Clark. The rider is a Spanish trader named Francis Vigo.

"'Everything is lost,' Vigo exclaims sadly. 'Hamilton has marched down from Detroit with British troops and Indians. Vincennes and Fort Sackville have fallen. In the spring Hamilton will attack the Kentucky settlements.'

"Clark's eyes burn. His brilliant campaign has been for nothing. He clenches his fists. 'We'll attack,' he says.

"'Attack!' the trader cries. 'How can you attack? The prairie is flooded. The rivers are running over their banks.'

"'We'll attack,' Clark says quietly. 'We'll march, we'll wade, we'll swim!' Then he almost shouts. 'But, by thunder, we'll attack!'

"Vigo looks at Clark. 'It seemed impossible when you did it the first time. Perhaps you can do it again.'

"Clark nods. His mind is already moving ahead to plan the attack. He turns and walks out into the night. He mutters to himself, 'I must do it again.'

"We left Kaskaskia on the afternoon of February 5. I was only seventeen at the time. But there was a younger soldier than I—the drummer boy, Willie Chalmers. He was only fourteen, and small for his age.

"Two companies of French militia had joined us. But we had only about a hundred and thirty men altogether.

"We struck out across the prairie. Then the rain began. It came down just as it's coming down tonight. Soon there wasn't a dry thread on our bodies.

"The next day and the next were the same. We forgot we had ever been warm and dry. We were half frozen. The men would mutter among themselves. 'We'll never get to Vincennes,' one would say. 'And if we did, this is not the time to attack,' another would answer.

"At such times Clark would cry out, 'No, no! Believe me. This is just the time to attack. The British don't believe we can get to them!'

"His own spirit never flagged. 'You're the best army a man ever led,' he'd say. 'I wouldn't trade you Long Knives for a thousand ordinary soldiers.' And the men would take heart.

"After eight days we came to the Little Wabash River. It looked as if we were through—the river was a raging torrent. East and west it had over-flowed its banks. And we were still over sixty miles from Vincennes.

"Colonel Clark sent for Willie Chalmers. The men were tired and cold and wet. They began to mutter again. Some said we couldn't go on.

"Clark stood for a moment and looked out over the raging water. Then suddenly he lifted the drummer boy, Willie Chalmers, onto the shoulders of one of his tallest men. He didn't say anything. He and the soldier just stepped forward into the icy water. Willie began to beat a fierce tattoo on his drum.

"The men saw Colonel Clark and the soldier and Willie heading into the river. Something came over their faces. I guess it was what you'd call inspiration. Anyway, a shout went up. And we all plunged into the river behind the Colonel and Willie and the soldier.

"The river got deeper and deeper, colder and colder. We could hardly keep our footing. Some of us stumbled and fell into the water.

"Then I heard someone laughing. I couldn't imagine what there might be to laugh about in the middle of an icy river. Then I saw Willie floating on his drum. He was still beating away on the rim of it, though his fingers were stiff. In spite of my chattering teeth, I laughed, too.

"We all plunged into the river behind the Colonel and
Willie and the soldier."

"For five long miles we waded through that
freezing flood. I don't think Willie stopped beating
on his drum once. Then Clark turned and said,
'Men, we can't turn back now. We've come this far.
We've got to go on!'

"The shivering, tired-out Long Knives cheered.

'On to Vincennes!' we cried.

"So it went, day after day, through mud and water. We ran out of food. And then we came to a bigger river, the Wabash itself.

"We were only nine miles below Vincennes, but it might as well have been ninety. We couldn't wade across the Wabash. It was too wide and deep. Again the men lost heart.

"But once more Clark rallied us. He set men to making a dugout from a tree trunk. Some French Canadians came down the river. Were they surprised to see us! They said they had passed two Indian canoes adrift in the river farther upstream. I was in the party that went to get them. But we found only one.

"That canoe and the dugout ferried back and forth across the Wabash, till all of us were on the other side. Then we pitched camp and slept.

"Next morning we were on our way. Clark said, 'In two hours we should see the rooftops of Vincennes.'

"That gave us new vigor. Weary, ragged, hungry, we followed him on.

"Unexpectedly we came across a group of duck hunters from Vincennes and captured one of them. He was dumfounded. He could hardly believe that we had made that march across the flooded prairie. The Colonel sent word by him to the French in the town.

"Those good people said nothing about us to the British garrison. They were loyal to us. And when we crept into the village that night, the housewives had a hot supper ready for us.

"After we had eaten, we opened fire on the fort. Hamilton and his men were completely surprised. We kept up our fire all night.

"Clark would move groups of us around to fire
from different directions."

"Clark would move groups of us around to fire from different directions. And he told us to laugh and holler at the top of our voices everywhere we went. The British thought they were surrounded by a large army.

"We took a little rest after four in the morning, and then started shooting again. In daylight the British could see better what was going on. But so could we. Every time a soldier in Fort Sackville would open a loophole to fire a gun, our long Kentucky rifles would speak first. It must have been right discouraging for them.

"As a matter of fact, Hamilton had all the advantage. He had almost as many men as we did, if he had only known it. He had cannon, and of course we didn't. He was behind fortification, while we had to use whatever cover we could find.

"But Hamilton had lost his nerve. At nine o'clock he asked for a truce.

"Hamilton and Clark talked several times throughout the day. Clark demanded unconditional surrender. He didn't want to yield an inch. Hamilton couldn't quite bring himself to give in. Every time the talks broke off, we would start firing again.

"Finally, at ten o'clock the next morning, Hamilton surrendered the fort and all his men.

"When the British soldiers filed out of Fort Sackville to lay down their arms, the French cheered. 'Long live the Americans!' they shouted. And Willie Chalmers beat his drum as he had never beaten it before."

What Happened Next?

• George Rogers Clark's victory at Vincennes gave America control of the Northwest Territory. The Great Lakes became the northern boundary of the United States and the Northwest Territory became the states of Ohio, Indiana, Illinois, Michigan, Wisconsin, and eastern Minnesota.

• Clark continued to lead military actions in the Northwest until the end of the War in 1783. He paid for many of them with his own funds and was never repaid by the government. As a result, he lived in poverty for the rest of his life.

• When the Revolutionary War ended, George retired to Clarksville, Indiana, which he had started in 1784 as the first English-speaking settlement in the old Northwest.

• After suffering a stroke in 1809, Clark moved in with his sister Lucy who lived in Locust Grove, near Louisville, Kentucky, which Clark had founded in 1778.

• He died in 1818. Thomas Jefferson said of Clark, "no man alive rated him higher than I did."

When George Rogers Clark Lived

Date	Event
1752	George Rogers Clark was born near Charlottesville, Virginia to John and Ann Rogers Clark.
1778	George Rogers Clark founded Louisville, Kentucky.
1779	British Governor Henry Hamilton surrendered to George Rogers Clark at the Battle of Vincennes, which won the Northwest Territory for the United States.
1784	George Rogers Clark founded Clarksville, Indiana.
1803	Clark retired to Clarksville, building a two-room cabin and operating a grist mill. George's younger brother, William, set off from George's cabin with Meriwether Lewis on the famous Lewis and Clark Expedition.
1818	Clark died at Locust Grove, home of his sister Lucy near Louisville, Kentucky.

Fun Facts About
George Rogers Clark

- George had five brothers and four sisters. Five of them served in the American Revolution and three of them became generals.

- When George Rogers Clark was born in 1752, George Washington was 20, John Adams was 17 and Daniel Boone was 18.

- In 1809, Clark suffered a stroke and fell into his cabin's fireplace. His leg was so badly burned that it had to be cut off. While the operation took place, George listened to the music of regimental fifes and drums. He had no anesthetic.

- With his victory that won the Northwest Territory, George Rogers Clark was responsible for doubling the size of the United States.

- In 1783, Thomas Jefferson asked George to head an expedition to explore the land west of the Mississippi. George declined. In 1803, Jefferson asked George's younger brother, William the same question and he accepted, becoming part of the famous Lewis and Clark expedition.

Visit www.patriapress.com/clark to learn more about George Rogers Clark.

About the Author

Katharine E. Wilkie was born in Lexington, KY. A teacher of English and History for most of her life, she wrote more than 20 books for children, including 8 in the *Childhood of Famous Americans Series.*™